9

JUNIOR

CLASSICS

Published in Red Turtle by
Rupa Publications India Pvt. Ltd 2016
7/16, Ansari Road, Daryaganj
New Delhi 110002

Sales centres:
Allahabad Bengaluru Chennai
Hyderabad Jaipur Kathmandu
Kolkata Mumbai

ISBN: 978-81-291-3893-4

Second impression 2017

10 9 8 7 6 5 4 3 2

Printed at Rakmo Press Pvt. Ltd, New Delhi

Contents

Pride and Prejudice

Jane Austen

It is a well-known fact that a single man in possession of a good fortune is always on a lookout for a beautiful wife.

However little is known about the feelings and views of the single man, this fact is so set and rooted in the minds of the neighbours, as he is regarded as the rightful property for one of their daughters.

Nowhere had it created more excitement and hope, than in the household of the Bennets, the chief residents of Longbourn.

'My dear Mr Bennet,' said Mrs Bennet. 'Have you heard that the posh Netherfield Park has been leased at last?'

'I have not,' replied Mr Bennet.

'Do you know who has taken it?' cried Mrs Bennet.

'I have no objection to hearing the name,' said Mr Bennet.

'It has been taken by a young man called Bingley,' said Mrs Bennet.

'Is he single or married?' asked Mr Bennet.

'Oh, single and has a huge fortune. What a fine thing for our girls!' said Mrs Bennet.

Mr Bennet was witty and intelligent and he was such a mixture of sarcastic humour, reserve

and impulse that the experience of twenty-three years had been insufficient to make his wife understand his character. She was a woman of mean understanding, little information and uncertain temper. Mr and Mrs Bennet had five unmarried daughters: Jane, Elizabeth, Mary, Kitty and Lydia. The business of her life was to get her daughters married; its solace was visiting and news.

Before long, a rumour circulated that Mr Bingley was to attend the forthcoming ball at the assembly rooms. He was to bring four people with him to the assembly.

The evening set for the ball came at last; when Bingley's party entered the assembly room it consisted of Mr Bingley, his two sisters, the husband of the eldest and another young man.

Mr Bingley was good-looking and gentleman-like; he had a pleasant expression; and easy, charming manners. His sisters were fine women, who were always dressed fashionably. His brother-in-law, Mr Hurst, merely looked the gentleman; but his friend Mr Darcy soon drew the attention of the room by his fine, tall, handsome features, and the report which was in general circulation within five minutes after his entrance, of his earning ten thousand pounds a year. The ladies declared he was much handsomer than Mr Bingley, and he was looked at with great admiration for about half the evening, till his manners gave a disgust which turned the tide of his popularity; for he was discovered to be proud.

Mr Bingley had soon introduced himself to all the well-known people in the room; he danced with everybody. Mr Darcy danced only once with Mrs Hurst and once with Miss Bingley, declined being introduced to any other lady, and spent the rest of the evening in walking about the room, speaking occasionally to one of his own party. What a contrast between him and his friend!

Elizabeth Bennet had been obliged, by the scarcity of gentlemen, to sit down for two

into interest. He was marvelling at the beautiful expression of her black eyes.

Miss Bingley said to Mr Darcy, 'How long has Elizabeth Bennet been your favourite? She is one of those young ladies who seek to recommend themselves to the other men by holding in their own low esteem.'

'Undoubtedly,' replied Darcy, 'there is malice in all the arts which ladies sometimes stoop to employ for captivation.'

Miss Bingley was not entirely satisfied with this reply, she decided to end the conversation and retire for the day. Next morning, Elizabeth

and Jane returned home. Darcy was glad to see them off, as Elizabeth fascinated him 'more than he liked'.

Though Elizabeth was clueless of Darcy's attachment towards her; her prejudice against him got far more pronounced and reinforced. One day, she met a handsome young man named Wickham, an officer

'I would not be so fussy as you are,' cried Mr Bingley, 'for a kingdom! Upon my honour, I never met with so many pleasant girls in my life as I have this evening; and there are several of them you see uncommonly pretty.'

'You are dancing with the only beautiful girl in the room,' said Mr Darcy, looking at the eldest Miss Bennet.

'Oh! She is the most beautiful creature I have ever seen! But there is one of her sisters sitting down just behind you, who is very pretty, and I dare say very agreeable. Do let me ask my partner to introduce you,' said Mr Bingley.

'Which one do you mean?' and turning round he looked for a moment at Elizabeth, till catching her eye, he withdrew his own and coldly said, 'She is tolerable, but not adorable enough to tempt me; I am in no humour at present to give consequence to young ladies who are slighted by other men. You had better return to your partner and enjoy her smiles, for you are wasting your time with me.'

Mr Bingley followed his advice. Mr Darcy walked off; and Elizabeth remained with not very cordial feelings towards him. She told the story, however, with great spirit among her friends; for she had a lively, playful disposition, which delighted in anything ridiculous.

The ladies of Longbourn wished to be acquainted with Jane. Mrs Hurst and her sister admired Jane and liked her, and pronounced her to be a sweet girl, and one whom they would want to know more of, though they found the mother to be intolerable, and the younger sisters not worth speaking to. Bingley felt authorized by such approval.

Before long, the Bingley sisters sent an invitation to Jane. Mrs Bennet was planning to send Jane by horse rather than coach, knowing that it would rain and that Jane therefore would have to spend the night at Mr Bingley's house. The plan went off too well. Jane had not been gone long before it started raining hard and hence could not come back.

The next day, Jane sent a letter for Elizabeth describing her state of health. Elizabeth, feeling really anxious, was determined to go to her. She was shown into the breakfast-parlour, where all except Jane were assembled. Elizabeth was glad to be taken to her immediately and Jane was delighted at her entrance. In the afternoon, Elizabeth felt that she must go but Jane was so bothered in parting with her, that Miss Bingley was obliged to convert the offer of the carriage to an invitation to remain at Netherfield Park for the present. Elizabeth most thankfully agreed, and a servant was dispatched to Longbourn to acquaint the family with her stay and bring back a supply of clothes.

At dinner, Mr Bingley's anxiety for Jane was evident. She had very little notice from any but him.

When dinner was over, Miss Bingley returned directly to Jane, and began abusing her as soon as she was out of the room. Her manners were pronounced to be very bad indeed, a mixture of pride and rudeness; she had no conversation, no style, no beauty. Mrs Hurst thought the same, and added,

'She has nothing, in short, to recommend her, but being an excellent walker. I shall never forget her appearance this morning. She really looked almost wild.'

As for Mr Darcy, the lack of feeling that he had felt initially for Elizabeth was changing dances; and during that time, Mr Darcy had been standing near her, close enough for her to hear a conversation between him and Mr Bingley, who came from the dance for a few minutes, to press his friend to join it.

'Come, Darcy,' said he, 'I must have you dance. I hate to see you standing about by yourself in this stupid manner. You had much better dance.'

'I certainly shall not. You know how I hate it, unless I am particularly acquainted with my partner. At such an assembly as this it would be insupportable. Your sisters are engaged, and there is not another woman in the room whom it would not be a punishment to me to stand up with.'

of the militia regiment quartered at Meryton, the nearest town to Longbourn. He disclosed to her that he was the son of a reliable steward of Darcy's father and how Darcy had mistreated him.

Later, at another ball thrown by Mr Bingley at Netherfield, Elizabeth felt that her family could have played their parts in the ball with more spirit and in a finer way.

The next morning his daughters returned from Netherfield.

'I hope, my dear,' said Mr Bennet to his wife, as they were at breakfast the next morning, 'that you have ordered a good dinner today, because I have reason to expect an addition to our family.'

Mrs Bennet's eyes sparkled.

'A gentleman and a stranger! It is Mr Bingley, I am sure! Well, I am sure I shall be extremely glad to see Mr Bingley.'

'It is not Mr Bingley,' said her husband, 'it is a person whom I never saw in the whole course of my life.'

This roused a general astonishment and he had the pleasure of being eagerly questioned by his wife and his five daughters at once.

After amusing himself some time with their curiosity, he thus explained,

'About a month ago I received this letter; and about a fortnight ago I answered it, for I thought it a case of some delicacy, and requiring early attention. It is from my cousin, Collins, who, when I am dead, may turn you all out of this house as soon as he pleases.'

'Oh! My dear,' cried his wife, 'I cannot bear to hear that mentioned. Pray do not talk of that horrible man. I do think it is the hardest thing in the world, that your estate should be disinherited from your own children; and I am sure, if I had been you, I should have tried long ago to do something or other about it.'

'At four o'clock, we may expect this peace-making gentleman,' said Mr Bennet.

Collins was punctual and was received with great politeness by the whole family. He was a tall, heavy-looking young man of twenty-five. His air was grave and stately, and his manners were very formal. He had not been long seated before he complimented Mrs Bennet on having so fine a family of daughters; said he had heard much of their beauty.

Having now a good house and a very sufficient income, he intended to marry; he had a wife in view, he meant to choose one of the daughters.

The next morning, in a tête-à-tête with Mrs Bennet and her family before breakfast, he realized that Jane, whom he had fixed his eyes on, was going to be engaged, and he had only to change from Jane to Elizabeth.

It was soon done. The next day, in a long, set speech Mr Collins proposed to Elizabeth and explained the reasons for marrying.

'My reasons for marrying are, first, that I think it a right thing for every clergyman to set the example of matrimony in his parish; secondly, I am convinced that it will add very greatly to my happiness. I shall be uniformly silent; and you may assure yourself that no censure and criticism shall ever pass my lips when we are married.'

It was absolutely necessary to interrupt him now.

'You are too hasty, sir,' she cried. 'You forget that I have made no answer. Let me do it without further loss of time. I am very sensible of the honour of your proposal but it is impossible for me to do otherwise than to decline them.'

Mrs Bennet, who considered a match between her daughter and Mr Collins as beneficial, was enraged. But Mrs Bennet did not give up. She talked to Elizabeth repeatedly; coaxed and threatened her by turns. She attempted to secure Jane in her interest, but Jane, with all possible mildness, declined interfering; and Elizabeth, sometimes with real earnestness, and sometimes with playful gaiety, replied to her attacks.

While the family were in this confusion, Elizabeth's friend, Charlotte Lucas came to spend the day with them. With Mr Collins heartbroken, he took no time to talk to Charlotte and one day proposed to her. She accepted his proposal and married him. Elizabeth was shocked, despite Charlotte's persistence that the match was the best for which she could hope. Mrs Bennet, of course, was furious with her daughter. She complained bitterly of all this to her husband.

'Indeed, Mr Bennet,' said she, 'it is very hard to think that Charlotte Lucas should ever be mistress of this house, that I should be forced to make way for her, and live to see her take her place in it!'

'My dear, do not give way to such gloomy thoughts. Let us hope for better things,' said Mr Bennet.

As the days passed, there was no communication from Bingley; and Jane's marriage prospects, too, were beginning to fade away.

Miss Bingley's letter arrived, and put an end to doubt. The very first sentence conveyed the assurance of their being all settled in London for the winter, and concluded with her brother's regret at not having had the time to pay his respects to his friends in Hertfordshire before he left the country.

Hope was over, entirely over; and Jane found that Miss Darcy's praise occupied the chief of it. Caroline Bingley boasted joyfully of their increasing intimacy, and she wrote also with great pleasure of her brother's being an inmate of Mr Darcy's house.

Elizabeth, to whom Jane very soon communicated most of the stories, listened in silent indignation. Her heart was divided between concern for her sister, and resentment against all others.

Mr Bennet treated the matter differently.

'So, Elizabeth,' said he one day, 'your sister is crossed in love, I find. I congratulate her. Next to being married, a girl likes to be crossed a little in love now and then. It is something to think of, and it gives her a sort of distinction among her companions. When is your turn to come? You will hardly bear to be long outdone by Jane. Now is your time. There are officers enough in Meryton to disappoint all the young ladies in the country. Let Wickham be your man. He is a pleasant fellow, and would jilt you creditably.'

'Thank you, sir, but a less agreeable man would satisfy me. We must not all expect Jane's good fortune.'

March was to take Elizabeth to meet Collins at Hunsford. She had promised to pay her visit to Collins in March. She was to accompany Sir William Lucas, Charlotte's father, and his second daughter.

Mr Collins and Charlotte appeared at the door, and the carriage stopped at the small gate.

In a moment they were all out of the chaise, rejoicing at the sight of each other. Mrs Collins welcomed her friend with the liveliest pleasure, and Elizabeth was more and more satisfied with her visit when she found herself so affectionately received. She saw instantly that her cousin's manners were not altered by his marriage. They were taken into the house and he punctually repeated all his wife's offers of refreshment.

Once during a conversation, Wickham had revealed to Elizabeth that Mr Collins's employer, Lady Catherine was also Mr Darcy's aunt and that her daughter and Mr Darcy were to marry. The next day at Collins's house, she saw Lady Catherine and her daughter. The daughter was irritable. Elizabeth thought, 'Darcy is marrying such as an unappealing person.' Lady Catherine invited them to feast at Rosings, a stately home that surprised and amazed even Sir William Lucas with its magnificence and luxury.

Lady Catherine dominated at the dinner. After the meal, she grilled Elizabeth about her childhood and education and how badly she and her sisters grew up.

Sir William stayed only a week at Hunsford, and soon left. It was about a fortnight that Collins had visited Lady Catherine's estate, the Rosings. On the following morning he hastened to Rosings to pay his respects. There were two nephews of

Lady Catherine, for Mr Darcy had brought with him a Colonel Fitzwilliam, the younger son of his uncle Lord, and to the great surprise, when Mr Collins returned, the gentlemen accompanied him and met with Elizabeth and Charlotte.

Another invitation to Rosings followed, and Colonel Fitzwilliam pay special attention and interest to Elizabeth during the dinner. After the meal, she played the piano and poked fun at Darcy, informing Colonel Fitzwilliam of his bad behaviour at the Meryton ball, at which he refused to dance with her.

In the following weeks, Darcy often came to the parsonage. Charlotte had once or twice suggested to Elizabeth the possibility of his being partial to her, but Elizabeth always laughed at the idea; and Mrs Collins did not think it right to take up the subject again.

More than once did Elizabeth, in her ramble within the park, unexpectedly meet Mr Darcy. And all the time he met her, he always showed a great level of interest, but, Elizabeth who had heard from Colonel Fitzwilliam proof of her suspicion that it was Darcy who had convinced Bingley to give up Jane, was now only more furious against the man who had broken her sister's heart, and thus always repulsed the man.

One evening, while she was walking, she heard a voice calling out; it was Darcy.

'I have struggled. My feelings will not be repressed. You must allow me to tell you that I admire and love you.'

Elizabeth felt herself growing angrier every moment, yet she tried to the utmost to speak with composure when she said, 'You are mistaken, Mr Darcy, if you suppose that the mode of your declaration affected me in any way other than to feel no guilt in refusing you.'

She saw him start at this, but he said nothing, and she continued, 'You could not have made the offer of your hand in any possible way that would have tempted me to accept it. You ruined the happiness of my sister, Jane and blighted the career of my friend, Wickham.' Saying this Elizabeth hurried away from Darcy.

Soon after, the next day, he met Elizabeth in the park and handed her a letter.

'Two offenses of a very different nature, and by no means of equal magnitude, you yesterday laid to my charge. In separating Bingley from Jane I had not the slightest notion that I was doing the latter any injury, since he never credited her with any strong attachment and Wickham had always been an idle and dissipated person. I had fulfilled my father's wishes and Wickham had repaid my generosity by trying to elope with my younger sister, Georgiana.'

Elizabeth was shocked by these revelations, and she thought, 'I was probably wrong to trust the officer.' She was in a state of flux.

Darcy and Colonel Fitzwilliam left Rosings. A week later, Elizabeth left too. When she reached London, she told Jane about Darcy's proposal and Wickham's real character but suppressed everything that pertained to her.

Lydia was invited to spend the summer in Brighton by the wife of a Colonel Forster. Mr Bennet let her go. The separation between her and her family was rather noisy than pathetic. The other sisters shed tears, but they did weep from vexation and envy. When Lydia went away she promised to write very often and very detailed letters to her mother, but her letters were always long expected, and always very short.

Some two months later, in July, Elizabeth accompanied the Gardiners, her aunt and uncle, on a tour of the Derbyshire countryside, and their travels took them close to Darcy's manor, Pemberley. As they turned in at the lodge, her spirits were in a high flutter. When they reached the place, they were admitted into the hall; they waited for the housekeeper. A housekeeper came, a respectable-looking elderly woman. They followed her into the dining parlour. It was a large room, handsomely fitted up.

'And of this place,' thought she, 'I might have been a mistress!'

She yearned to inquire of the housekeeper whether her master was really absent, but had not the courage for it. However, when the question was asked by her uncle, Mrs Reynolds said, 'We expect him tomorrow, with a large party of friends.'

'He is the best landlord, and the best master,' said she, 'that ever lived; not like the wild young men nowadays, who think of nothing but themselves. There is not one of his tenants or servants who will not call him a good person. Some people call him proud, but I am sure I never saw anything of it.'

Elizabeth was in awe to hear such a wonderful description of a man whom she considered unbearably arrogant.

The next day, Darcy and his sister appeared at Elizabeth's inn and then Darcy introduced his sister to Elizabeth. To her astonishment, she found her new acquaintance as embarrassed as she was. They had not been together for a long time, when Darcy told Elizabeth that Mr Bingley was waiting to meet her.

'It is a very long time since I had had the pleasure of seeing Jane,' Bingley said. And, before she could reply, he added, 'It is more than eight months. We have not met since the 26th of November, when we were all dancing together at Netherfield.'

It was not often she could turn her eyes towards Darcy and whenever she could, she did catch a glimpse of him. The visitors stayed at the inn for a half an hour. When they arose to depart, Mr Darcy called on his sister to join him in expressing their wish of seeing Mr and Mrs Gardiner, and Miss Bennet, to dinner at Pemberley, before they left the country.

The next day, on reaching the house, they were received by Miss Darcy, who was sitting there with Mrs Hurst and Miss Bingley. Miss Bingley said with sneering civility, 'Pray, Miss Eliza, are not the—shire Militia removed from Meryton? They must be a great loss to your family.'

After they left, Mr Darcy followed them to their carriage; Miss Bingley was venting her feelings in criticism on Elizabeth's personality, behaviour and dress. But Georgiana would not join her.

When Darcy returned, Miss Bingley could not help repeating to him some part of what she had been saying to his sister.

'How very ill Miss Eliza Bennet looks this morning, Mr Darcy!' she cried. 'I never in my life saw anyone so much altered as she is since the winter. She is grown so brown and coarse!'

'Yes,' replied Darcy, who could contain himself no longer, 'but that was only when I first saw her, for it is many months since I have considered her as one of the handsomest women of my acquaintance.'

He then went away.

When Elizabeth returned to her inn, she found two letters from Jane. The first letter read: 'Something has occurred of the most unexpected and serious nature; but I am afraid of alarming you—be assured that we are all well. What I have to say relates to poor Lydia. A message came at twelve last night, just as we were all gone to bed, from Colonel Forster, to inform us that Lydia was gone off to Scotland with one of his officers; to own the truth, with Wickham!'

Elizabeth on finishing the first letter instantly seized the other, and opening it with the utmost impatience, read as follows: 'And the couple instead of going to Scotland to get married were believed to be living together in London unmarried.'

As Elizabeth darted out to find the Gardiners, Darcy appeared and she told him the story. Darcy immediately held himself responsible for not exposing Wickham and Elizabeth blamed herself for the same reason. She decided to leave for Longbourn immediately.

On reaching Longbourn, they found that Mr Bennet had left for London in search for Lydia and Wickham. Mrs Bennet was obviously frenzied and frantic, blaming Colonel Forster for not taking care of her daughter.

Mrs Gardiner followed Mr Bennet to London and wrote letters to the Bennets to inform them about the whereabouts of the couple. And each time he wrote about the search being unsuccessful. At last, Mr Bennet decided to return home. Two days after Mr Bennet returned to Longbourn, Mr Gardiner wrote that the couple had been found.

He further wrote that Wickham said, 'I would marry Lydia, if the Bennets would assure and promise me a small income.'

Mr Bennet gladly agreed, deciding that marriage to a crook is better than a ruined reputation.

Wickham and Lydia were married and the young couple were received with open arms at Longbourn.

'Well, Mamma,' said Lydia. 'What do you think about my husband? Is he not a charming man. I think all my sisters should go to Brighton to get husbands.'

'Thank you for your share of concern,' said Elizabeth, 'but I don't like your way of getting husbands.'

'But I must tell you how it went off. We were married, you know, at St Clement. Mr Darcy had done so well,' said Lydia.

'Mr Darcy!' repeated Elizabeth, in utter amazement. Mr Darcy had been at her sister's wedding.

She immediately wrote a letter to Mr Gardiner to confirm her suspicion. And she immediately received some information, which convinced her of his presence.

Darcy on hearing about the elopement immediately left for London. Darcy, thanks to his knowledge of Wickham's history, found out where Lydia and Wickham were residing. And by paying amount to the tune of thousand pounds, he persuaded him to make Lydia an honest woman. He literally bribed the man who he wished to avoid and whose very name was a punishment for him to pronounce.

Meanwhile, Bingley accompanied by Darcy made their appearance at Netherfield Park and at Bennets's house. They soon left, promising the Bennets that they would come back for dinner.

With time, Darcy and Elizabeth came to an understanding. Elizabeth gathered up courage one day and thanked Darcy for all he had done for Lydia.

'I would like to declare that whatever I did was only for you, Elizabeth.'

The Bennets were on cloud nine, when they first heard of the Elizabeth's news because they had practically seen nothing of the courtship.

Mr Bennet commented, 'Elizabeth, I have high regard for all my three son-in-laws, but I think I shall quite be fond of your husband quite as well as Jane's. If any men come for Mary and Kitty, send them in, I am quite at leisure.'

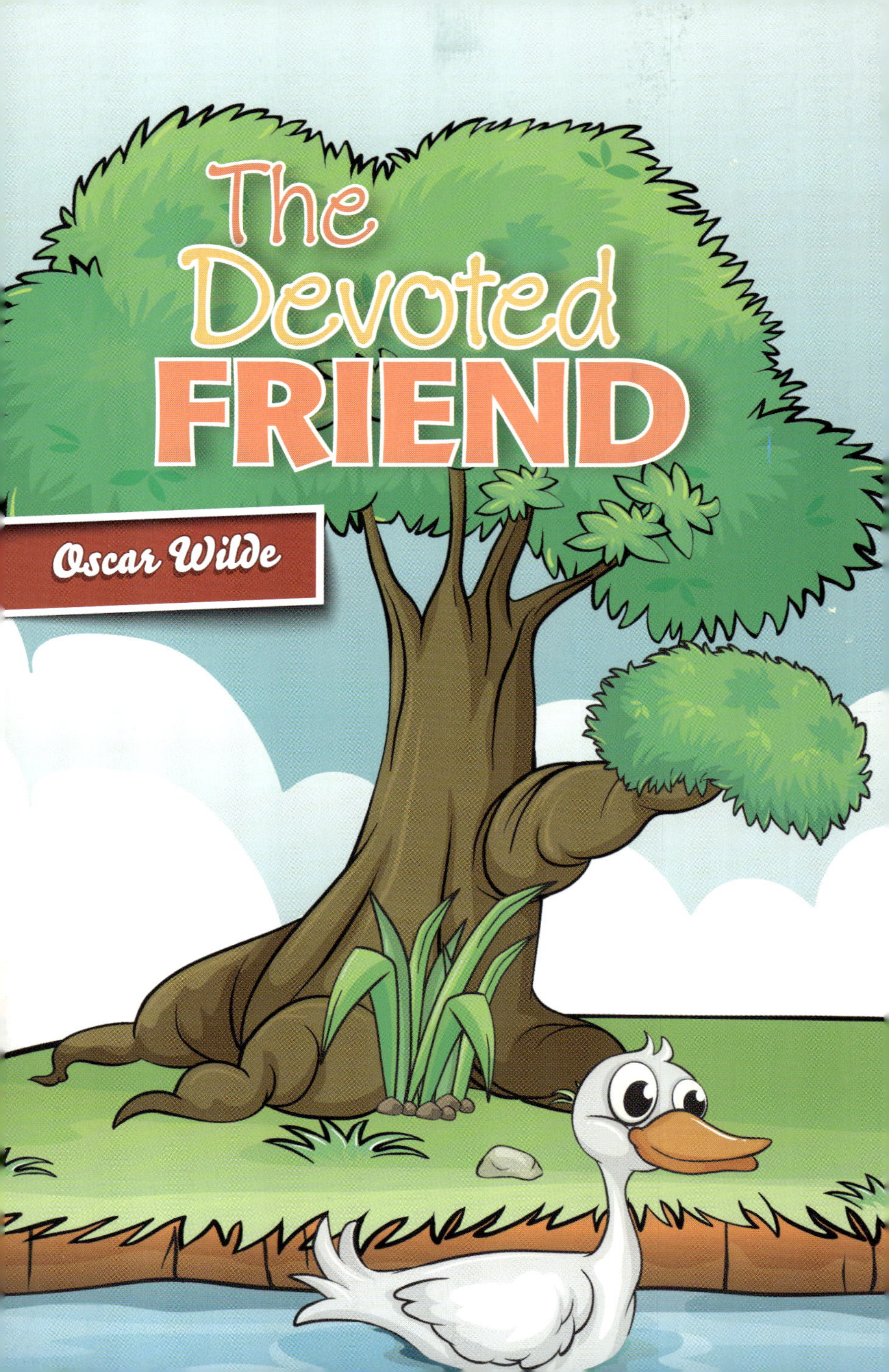

The Devoted
FRIEND
Oscar Wilde

Once there were two friends: a Green Linnet and a Water-rat. They were close yet they had different concepts of friendship. They had different opinions about who a real devoted friend could be and their argument would go on forever. Nevertheless, nothing, no hard feelings came in between their friendly relationship.

It was morning time. The old Water-rat sneaked his head out of a hole. He had bright beady eyes and stiff grey whiskers and his tail was like a long bit of black India-rubber. He saw little ducks swimming in the pool. The little ducks looked like many yellow canaries. Their mother, who was pure white with real red legs, was trying to teach them how to stand on their heads in the water.

'You will never be in the best society unless you can stand on your heads,' the mother duck kept saying to her little ones. Every now and then, she showed them how to stand on their head. However, her little ones never paid any attention to her. They were so young that they did not know and bother what an advantage it is to be in a good society.

'What disobedient children! They really deserve to be drowned,' cried the old Water-rat who had been observing the mother duck and her little ones.

'Nothing of the kind, everyone must make a beginning and parents cannot be too patient,' answered the Duck.

'Ah! I know nothing about the feelings of parents. I am not a family man. In fact, I have never been married, and I never intend to be. Love is all very well in its way, but friendship is much higher. Indeed, I know of nothing in the world that is either nobler or rarer than a devoted friendship,' said the Water-rat.

A Green Linnet, who was sitting in a willow-tree, overheard the conversation between the Water-rat and the Duck, cut him off, 'And what, pray, is your idea of the duties of a devoted friend?'

'Yes, this is just what I want to know,' said the Duck. She swam away to the end of the pond, and stood upon her head, with a sole intention to give her children a good example.

The Water-rat cried, 'What a silly question! I should expect my devoted friend to be devoted to me, of course.'

'And what would you do in return?' asked the little bird, swinging upon a silver spray, and flapping his tiny wings.

'I don't understand you,' answered the Water-rat.

'Let me narrate a story on the subject,' said the Linnet.

'Is the story about me?' asked the curious Water-rat, 'If so, I will listen to it, for I am extremely fond of fiction.'

'Yes, it is very much applicable to you,' answered the Linnet. He flew down, and alighted upon the bank and started telling the story of 'The Devoted Friend'.

'A long time ago, the lived an honest little fellow named Hans,' started the Linnet.

'Was he very distinguished?' asked the Water-rat.

'Not at all,' answered the Linnet. 'I don't think he was distinguished at all, except for his kind heart and his funny round good-humoured face. Hans lived in a tiny cottage all by himself, and every day he worked in his garden. In all the countryside there was no garden so lovely as his. Sweet-william grew there, and

gilly-flowers and shepherds-purses and fair-maids of France. There were damask roses, and yellow roses, lilac crocuses, and gold, purple violets and white. Columbine and ladysmock, marjoram and wild basil, the cowslip and the flower-de-luce, the daffodil and the clove-Pink bloomed or blossomed in their proper order as the months went by, one flower taking another flower's place, so that there were always beautiful things to look at, and pleasant to smell,' exaggerated the Linnet.

'Little Hans had a great many friends, but the most devoted friend of all was big Hugh the Miller. Indeed, so devoted was the rich Miller to little Hans, that he would never go by his garden without leaning over the wall and plucking a large nosegay, or a handful of sweet herbs, or filling his pockets with plums and cherries if it was the fruit season.

"My dear friend, in my humble opinion real friends should have everything in common," the Miller used to tell. All the while little Hans nodded and smiled, and felt very proud of having a friend with such noble ideas.

'It was indeed strange for the neighbours to find out that the rich Miller never gave little Hans anything in return. The Miller had hundred sacks of flour stored away in his mill, six cows, and a large flock of woolly sheep. Hans never even took the trouble to ask about his friend's possession or wealth. Nothing gave him greater pleasure than listening to all the wonderful things the Miller used to say about the unselfishness of true friendship,' carried on the Linnet.

'Little Hans always worked in his garden. He remained happy and contented during the spring, summer and the autumn. Nevertheless, when the winter came, he had no fruit or flowers to sell in the market. So, he suffered a good deal from cold and hunger. He often had to go to without any supper but a few dried pears or some hard nuts. He was extremely lonely during the winter season but his friend, the Miller never came to see him.

'On being asked by his wife to visit little Hans, the Miller told, "There is no good in visiting little Hans as long as the snow lasts, for when people are in trouble they should be left alone, and not be bothered by visitors. That is my idea about friendship, and I am sure I am right. So, I shall wait till the arrival of spring and then pay him a visit. He will be able to give me a large basket of primroses then and that will make him very happy."

'The Miller's wife encouraged her husband. She sat in her comfortable armchair by the big pinewood fire and said, "You are certainly very thoughtful about others, very thoughtful indeed. It is quite a treat to hear you talk about friendship. I am sure the clergyman could not say such beautiful things as you do, though he lives in a three-storied house, and wears a gold ring on his little finger."

"But father, could we not ask little Hans up here? If poor Hans is in trouble I will give him half my porridge, and show him my white rabbits," said the Miller's youngest son who was not like his parents.

"What a silly boy you are!" cried the Miller, "I really don't know what is the use of sending you to school. It seems that you have not learned anything. Why, if little Hans came up here, and saw our warm fire, our good supper and our great cask of red wine, he might get envious, and envy is the most terrible thing, and would spoil anybody's nature. I certainly will not allow Hans' nature to be spoiled. I am his best friend, and I will always watch over him, and see that he is not led into any temptations. Besides, if Hans came here, he might ask me to let him have some flour on credit, and that I could not do. Flour is one thing, friendship is another, and they should not be confused. Why, the words are spelt differently, and mean quite different things. Everybody can see that."

"Oh! How well you talk, my dear!" said the Miller's wife and she poured herself out a large glass of warm ale. "I really feel quite drowsy. It is just like being in church."

"Lots of people act well," answered the Miller, "but very few people talk well, which shows that talking is much more difficult thing of the two, and much the finer thing also." Having said so, he looked sternly across the table at his little son, who felt so ashamed of himself that he hung his head down, and grew quite scarlet, and began to cry into his tea'.

Here the Water-rat interrupted, 'Is that how the story ends?'

'Certainly not,' answered the Linnet, 'that is the beginning.'

'Then you are quite behind the age. Every good storyteller nowadays starts

with the end, and then goes on to the beginning, and concludes with the middle. That is the new method. I heard all about it the other day from a critic who was walking round the pond with a young man. He spoke of the matter at great length, and I am sure he must have been right, for he had blue spectacles and a baldhead, and whenever the young man made any remark, he always answered "Pooh!" However, pray go on with your story. I like the Miller immensely. I have all kinds of beautiful sentiments myself, so there is a great sympathy between us,' said the Water-rat.

The Linnet hopped on one leg and on the other and continued, 'As soon as the winter was over, the primroses began to open their pale yellow stars. The Miller told his wife that he would go down and see little Hans.'

"What a good heart you have!" cried the Miller's wife, "You always think of others. Please take the big basket with you for the flowers."

'The Miller tied the sails of the windmill together with a strong iron chain, and went down the hill with the basket on his arm. He saw little Hans and greeted him. Hans was happy to see his friend the Miller. The Miller asked Hans, "My friend how have you been all the winter?" Little Hans cried and told him how he had a hard time during winter season. Now that spring was around, he was quite happy with all his flowers doing well. The Miller tried to sound compassionate and told him how his family had talked about him during the winter.

"Oh! That was very kind of you. I was half afraid you had forgotten me," replied little Hans.

'The Miller tried to sound more compassionate and went on, "I am surprised at you. Friendship never forgets. That is the wonderful thing about it, but I am afraid you do not understand the poetry of life. How lovely your primroses are looking, by-the-by!"

"They are certainly very lovely," said Hans, "And it is the most lucky thing for me that I have so many. I am going to bring them into the market and sell them to the Burgomaster's daughter, and buy back my wheelbarrow with the money."

"Buy back your wheelbarrow? You don't mean to say you have sold it? What a very stupid thing to do!"

"Well, the fact is," said Hans, "that I was obliged to. You see the winter was a very bad time for me, and I really had no money at all to buy bread with. So I first sold the silver buttons off my Sunday coat, and then I sold my silver chain, then I sold my big pipe and at last I sold my wheelbarrow. But I am going to buy them all back again now."

"Hans, my friend," said the Miller, "I will give you my wheelbarrow. It is not in very good repair;

indeed, one side is gone, and there is something wrong with the wheel-spokes, but in spite of that I will give it to you. I know it is very generous of me, and a great many people would think me extremely foolish for parting with it, but I am not like the rest of the world. I think that generosity is the essence of friendship, and besides, I have a new wheelbarrow for myself. Yes, you may set your mind at ease; I will give you my wheelbarrow."

'Little Hans thought it was very generous of his friend to have presented the wheelbarrow to him. His funny round face glowed all over with pleasure. He told the Millers, "I can easily repair the wheelbarrow with a plank of wood in the house that I have."

"A plank of wood!" said the Miller. "Why that is just what I want for the roof of my barn. There is a very large hole in it, and the corn will all get damp if I don't stop it up. How lucky you mentioned it! It is quite remarkable how one good action always breeds another. I have given you my wheelbarrow, and now you are going to give me your plank. Of course, the wheelbarrow is worth far more than the plank, but true, friendship never notices things like that. Pray get it at once, and I will set to work at my barn this very day."

"Oh! Certainly, my friend!" cried little Hans, and he ran into the shed and dragged the plank out. The Miller looked at the plank and told Hans that it was not a very big plank. He made it clear that he would use the plank to mend his barn-roof. He was not yet satiated with his possession of the plank.

"My dear friend, I have given you my wheelbarrow, I am sure you would like to give me some flowers in return from your lovely garden. Here is the basket. Please fill it quite full," told the Miller to little Hans.

"Quite full?" said little Hans in quite a distressed tone. The basket was very big, and he knew that if he filled it full, he would have no flowers left to sell in the market, which means it would be hard to get his silver buttons back.

'The cunning Miller answered, "Well, my dear friend. As I have given you my wheelbarrow, I think it is not too much to ask you for a few flowers. I may be wrong, but I should have thought that friendship, true friendship, was quite free from selfishness of any kind.'

'Poor Hans, who was by now moved by the Miller's words, cried, "My dear friend, my best friend! You are welcome to all the flowers in my garden. I would much sooner have your good opinion that my silver buttons any day."

'No sooner than he said so, Hans ran and plucked all his pretty primroses, and filled the Miller's basket.

'The Miller said goodbye to little Hans and went up the hill with the plank on his shoulder, and the big basket full of primroses in his hand. Hans also wished his friend and began to dig away quite merrily. He was quite pleased about the wheelbarrow, which his friend, the Miller, had promised to give him.

'The next day Hans was busy nailing up some honeysuckle against the porch. All of a sudden, he heard his friend's voice calling to him from the road. Hans hastily jumped off the ladder, ran down the garden and looked over the wall. He saw his friend standing with a large sack of flour on his back.

'He called out to Hans and asked, "Dear little Hans, would you mind carrying this sack of flour for me to the market?"

'Little Hans replied, "Oh, I would love to but I am really busy today. I have got all my creepers to nail up and all my flowers to water, and all my grass to roll."

'The Miller put on an aggravated look and told Hans, 'I am going to give you my wheelbarrow considering you as my dear friend and it is rather unfriendly of you to refuse such a little help from your end.'

'Little Hans was quite saddened by his friend's words.

"Oh, don't say so my dear friend," cried little Hans.

'Next moment he ran in for his cap, and trudged off with the big sack on his shoulders.

'It was quite a hot day and the road to the market was terribly dusty. Before reaching the sixth milestone towards the market, he was so tired that he had to sit down and rest. He bravely went on and finally reached the market. He waited at the market for quite some time to sell away the sack of flour. After selling it for a very good price, he returned home at once. He did not think about staying back since he was afraid of being robbed on the way during the night.

'It was certainly a hard day for poor Hans but he was quite glad that he did not refuse his help to his friend the Miller who will give him his wheelbarrow.

'The next morning, the Miller came down from the hill to get his money for the sack of flour. Little Hans was still in bed as he was quite tired. The Miller addressed him as a lazy fellow.

'He told Hans, "Really considering that I am going to give you my wheelbarrow, I think you

might work harder. Idleness is a great sin, and I certainly don't like any of my friends to be idle or sluggish. You must not mind my speaking quite plainly to you. Of course, I should not dream of doing so if I were not your friend. But what is the good of friendship if one cannot say exactly what one means? Anybody can say charming things and try to please and to flatter, but a true friend always says unpleasant things, and does not mind giving pain. Indeed, if he is a really true friend he prefers it, for he knows that then he is doing well.'

'Little Hans was quite embarrassed by his friend's words. He woke up rubbing his eyes and pulled off his nightcap.

"But I was so tired that I thought I would lie in bed for a little time, and listen to the birds singing. Do you know that I always work better after hearing the birds sing?"

'The Miller clapped little Hans on the back and told him, "Well, I am glad for that but I want you to come up to the mill as soon as you are dressed, and mend my barn-roof for me."

'Poor Hans was anxious to go and work in his garden. His flowers had not been watered for two days. But he did not want to say no to his friend's request for he was such a good friend to him. In quite a shy and timid voice he asked the Miller if it would be unfriendly of him to say he was busy.

'The cunning Miller replied, "I do not think it is much to ask of you, considering that I am going to give you my wheelbarrow, but of course if you refuse I will go and do it myself."

'Poor Hans was moved again by his friend's words. He quickly jumped out of his bed, got ready and went up to the barn and worked there all day long until sunset. When it was almost dark, the Miller came to see how he was getting on. He asked Hans if he had mended the hole in the roof or not.

"It is quite mended," answered little Hans, climbing down the ladder. The Miller was quite delighted to know that the work was successfully done. He praised his friend for his effort.

"It gives me immense pleasure to hear you talk," said Hans sitting down and wiping his little forehead.

'The Miller recited his usual ideas about friendship to little Hans. He suggested Hans to take more pains. Now that his roof was mended, he suggested Hans to go home and rest for he wanted him to drive his sheep to the mountain the next day.

'Poor Hans was quite afraid to tell anything to the Miller. The next day, early in the morning, the Miller brought his sheep round to the cottage. Little Hans had no choice left so he started off with them to the mountain. It took him the whole day to reach the mountain. As he returned, we was so tired that we went off to sleep in his chair. The next day, he did not wake up till broad daylight.

'Once when he woke up, he thought he would spend a delightful time in his garden and he went to work at once. But alas! The Miller never gave him any chance to work in his garden. He would often come round and send him off on long errands or make him work at his mille. Tired and distressed, little Hans was quite worried about his flowers. He was sad for a while with the thought that his flowers might think he had forgotten them all. But the next moment, he consoled himself by the reflection that the Miller was his best friend and worth much more than his flowers. Besides, the Miller used to say he was going to give him his wheelbarrow and that, in his opinion, was an act of pure generosity.

'Little Hans kept on working for the Miller and the Miller would say all kinds of beautiful things about friendship, which Hans often noted down in a notebook and read over at night for he was a very good scholar. One night, as Little Hans

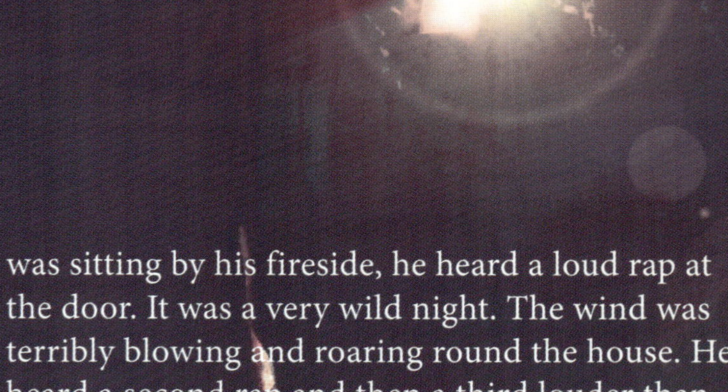

was sitting by his fireside, he heard a loud rap at the door. It was a very wild night. The wind was terribly blowing and roaring round the house. He heard a second rap and then a third louder than any of the others. He thought it was some poor traveller. Yet he saw the Miller with a lantern in one hand and a big stick in the other standing outside his cottage.

"Dear Little Hans, I am in great trouble," cried the Miller. "My little boy has fallen off a ladder and hurt himself, and I am going for the Doctor. However, he lives so far away, and it is such a bad night, that it has just occurred to me that it would be much better if you went instead of me. You know I am going to give you my wheelbarrow, and so, it is only fair that you should do something for me in return."

'Little Hans agreed to start off at once, though he asked the Miller to lend him his lantern as the night was so dark and that he was quite afraid to fall into the ditch.

'The Miller did not agree. He said it was his new lantern and it would be a great loss if anything happened to it.

'Poor Hans decided to start without the lantern. He took down his great fur coat and his warm scarlet cap, tied a muffler round his throat, and started. It was a dreadful storm and the night was scarily dark. Little Hans could hardly see anything. The wind was so strong that he could hardly stand. He gathered all his courage and walked about for three hours. He finally arrived at the Doctor's house and knocked at the door.

'The Doctor put his head out of his bedroom window and cried, "Who is there?"

'Little Hans replied it was him and explained how the Miller's son had fallen from a ladder and hurt himself. He also explained that the Miller wants him to come at once. The Doctor agreed to come along. He ordered his horse, his big boots and his lantern, came downstairs and rode off in the direction of the Miller's house. Little Hans was trudging behind him.

'The storm started getting worse and worse, and the rain started falling in torrents. Poor Hans could not see where he was going. He could not keep up with the Doctor's horse. At last, he lost his way and wandered off on the moor. The moor was a dangerous place full of deep holes. Poor little Hans was drowned there. The next day, his lifeless body was found floating in a great pool of water by some goatherds. His body was brought back to the cottage.

'Everybody went to little Han's funeral, as he was so popular for his act of bravery and generosity. The Miller was the chief mourner.

"As I was his best friend," said the Miller, "it is only fair that I should have the best place." So he walked at the head of the procession in a long black cloak, and every now and then he wiped his eyes with a big pocket-handkerchief.

"Little Hans is certainly a great loss to everyone," said the Blacksmith. When the funeral was over, all of them were comfortably seated in the inn. They drank spiced wine and ate sweet cakes.

'The Miller grieved how Hans was a great loss to him at any rate. He said, "Why, I had as good as given him my wheelbarrow, and now I really don't know what to do with it. It is very much in my way at home, and it is in such bad repair that I could not get anything for it if I sold it. I will certainly take care not to give away anything again."'

In that instant, the Water-rat, after a long pause said, 'Well?'

'Well, that is the end of the story,' said the Linnet.

The Water-rat asked what became of the Miller to which the Linnet replied he did not know and he did not care either. The Water-rat cried how it was evident that the Linnet had no sympathy in his nature.

'I am afraid you don't quite see the moral of the story,' said the Linnet.

'The what?' said the Water-rat.

'The moral,' said the Linnet again.

'Do you mean to say that the story has a moral?' asked the Water-rat putting on a curious look.

'Certainly,' said the Linnet.

The Water-rat became very angry. 'I think you should have told me that before you began. If you had done so, I certainly would not have listened to you.'

The Duck paddled up some minutes afterwards and asked the Linnet how he found the Water-rat. She said, 'He has a great many good points, but for my own part I have a mother's feelings, and I can never look at a confirmed bachelor without the tears coming into my eyes.'

'I am rather afraid that I have annoyed him,' answered the Linnet. 'The fact is that I told him a story with a moral.'

'Ah! That is always a very dangerous thing to do,' said the Duck.

The Linnet could not agree more with the Duck.

THE GOLD BUG

Edgar Allan Poe

What ho! What ho! This fellow is dancing mad! He hath been bitten by the Tarantula.

All in the Wrong.

Many years ago, I developed a friendship with a Mr William Legrand. He was from an ancient Huguenot family, and had once been wealthy, but a series of misfortunes had reduced him to want and so he left New Orleans, the city of his forefathers, and took up his residence at Sullivan's Island, near Charleston, South Carolina.

This island is a very singular one stretching about three miles long with very little vegetation and is separated from the main land by a small creek. With the exception of a few palms in the western point and white beach on the seacoast, the island is covered with a dense undergrowth of sweet myrtles.

In the inner part, not far from the eastern end of the island, Legrand had built himself a small hut. He was a well-educated man but infected with misanthropy, and often had contrary mood swings. His chief amusements were fishing and exploring the island in search for shells or other insect specimens. In the trips he was usually accompanied by an old man, called Jupiter, who had been freed from slavery before the reverses

of the family, yet chose to remain with his young 'Massa Will.'

About the middle of October 18—, on an unexpected chilly day, I visited Legrand, whom I had not visited for several weeks. Upon reaching the hut I rapped, as was my custom, and getting no reply, searched for the key where I knew it was hidden, and let myself in. A fine fire was blazing on the hearth. I threw off my overcoat, took an armchair by the crackling logs, and waited the arrival of my hosts.

Soon after dark they arrived, and gave me a most cordial welcome. Jupiter busied himself to prepare supper while Legrand enthusiastically told me about the day's events. He had found and secured, with Jupiter's assistance, a scarabaeus, which he believed to be a new species, and in respect to which he wished to have my opinion on the next day.

'And why not tonight?' I asked, unable to hide my curiosity.

'Ah, if I had only known you were here!' said Legrand. 'As I was coming home I met Lieutenant G—, and, very foolishly, I lent him the bug, so it will be impossible for you to see it until morning. It is of a brilliant gold colour about the size of a large hickory-nut, with two jet black spots near one extremity of the back, and another, somewhat longer, at the other. The antennae are—'

'I have been telling you, Massa Will,' said Jupiter, 'that bug is a gold bug. Each part is solid except its wing. I have never seen such a heavy bug.'

'Well, suppose it is, Jup,' Legrand earnestly replied. 'The colour,' here he turned to me, 'is really almost enough to justify Jupiter's idea. You never saw a more brilliant metallic lustre than the scales emit. I can give you some idea of the shape.'

Saying this, he seated himself at a small table, on which were a pen and ink, but no paper. He looked for some in a drawer, but found none.

'Never mind,' said he at length, 'this will do.' And he drew from his waistcoat pocket a scrap and made upon it a rough drawing with the pen. While he did this, I retained my seat by the fire, for it was still chilly. When the design was complete, he handed it to me without rising. As I received it, Legrand's large Newfoundland, rushed in, leaped upon my shoulders and loaded me with caresses; for I had shown him much attention during previous visits. I looked at the paper, and, to speak the truth, found myself puzzled at what my friend had depicted.

'Well!' I said, after contemplating it for some minutes, 'this is a strange bug, I must confess: never saw anything like it before—unless it was a skull, or a death's-head—which it more nearly resembles than anything else that has come under my observation.'

'A death's-head!' said he, a little irritated. 'I draw quite fine—should do it at least—have had good masters.'

'But, my dear fellow, you are joking then,' said I, 'this is clearly a skull and your scarabaeus must be the most unique scarabaeus in the world if it resembles it. But where are the antennae you spoke of?'

'I am sure you must see the antennae. I made them as distinct as they are in the original insect.'

'Well, well,' I said, 'perhaps you have, still I don't see them.'

I was surprised at the turn of affairs; his ill humour puzzled me and, as for the drawing of the beetle, there were positively no antennae visible, and the whole did bear a very close resemblance to a death's-head.

He received the paper very fretfully, and was about to crumple it, apparently to throw it in the fire, when a casual glance at the design suddenly drew his attention. In an instant, his face grew violently red. For some minutes, he continued to scrutinize the drawing minutely where he sat. At last he arose, took a candle from the table and anxiously examined the paper; turning it in all directions. Presently he took from his coat pocket a wallet, placed the paper carefully in it, and deposited both in a writing desk, which he locked. As the evening wore away, his enthusiasm had disappeared and he seemed preoccupied in his own thoughts. Seeing my host in this mood, I felt it proper to take leave.

A month after this (and during the interval I had seen nothing of Legrand) I received a visit, at Charleston, from his man, Jupiter. I had never seen him look so dispirited, and I feared that some serious disaster had befallen my friend.

Upon my enquiry, Jupiter reported that Legrand has not been himself lately, that he is pale and walks about with his head down, and continually works with figures on a slate. Legrand had been talking about gold in his sleep as well. Jupiter thinks that his prized beetle bit him and infected him with a desire for gold.

Jupiter, then, handed me a note, which ran thus:

> *My DEAR—*
>
> *Why have I not seen you for so long a time? I hope you have not been so foolish as to take offence at my behaviour the other day.*
>
> *Since I saw you I have had great cause for anxiety. I have something to tell you, yet scarcely know how to tell it, or whether I should tell it at all.*
>
> *I have not been quite well for some days past, and poor old Jup annoys me, almost beyond endurance, by his well-meant intentions. Would you believe it?—he had prepared a huge stick, the other day, with which to chastise me for giving him the slip, and spending the day, alone, among the hills on the main land. I verily believe that my ill looks alone saved me a flogging.*
>
> *I have made no addition to my cabinet since we met.*
>
> *If you can, in any way, make it convenient, come over with Jupiter. Do come. I wish to see you tonight, upon business of importance. I assure you that it is of the highest importance.*
>
> *Ever yours,*
>
> WILLIAM LEGRAND.

There was something in the tone of this note, which gave me great uneasiness and without a moment's hesitation, I prepared to accompany Jupiter.

Upon reaching the creek, I noticed a scythe and spades, all apparently new, lying in the boat in which we were to embark.

I queried for their purpose, to which Jupiter replied that he purchased them at his master's order but did not know for what purpose.

It was about three in the afternoon when we arrived. Legrand had been awaiting us in eager expectation. He grasped my hand with a nervous cordiality, which alarmed me and

strengthened the suspicions already entertained. After some enquiries about his health, I asked him, if he had yet obtained the scarabaeus from Lieutenant G—.

'Oh, yes,' he replied, 'I got it back the other day. Nothing should tempt me to part with that scarabaeus. Do you know that Jupiter is quite right about it?'

'In what way?' I asked.

'In supposing it to be a bug of real gold.'

He said this with an air of profound seriousness, and I felt inexpressibly shocked.

'This bug is to make my fortune,' he continued, with a triumphant smile, 'to reinstate me in my family possessions.'

Hereupon Legrand arose and brought me the beetle from a glass case in which it was enclosed. It was a beautiful scarabaeus, and, at that time, unknown to naturalists—of course a great prize in a scientific point of view. There were two round, black spots near one extremity of the back, and a long one near the other. The scales were exceedingly hard and glossy, with all the appearance of burnished gold. The weight of the insect was very remarkable.

'I sent for you so that I might have your counsel and assistance in furthering the views of Fate and of the bug.'

'My dear Legrand,' I cried, interrupting him, 'you are certainly unwell, and you better take some precautions. You shall go to bed, and I will remain with you a few days, until you get over this. You are feverish and…'

'Feel my pulse,' said he.

I felt it, and found not the slightest indication of fever.

'Jupiter and myself are going upon an expedition into the hills, upon the main land, and, in this expedition, we shall need the aid of some person whom we can confide. You are the only one we can trust.'

'I am anxious to oblige you in any way,' I replied, 'but do you mean to say

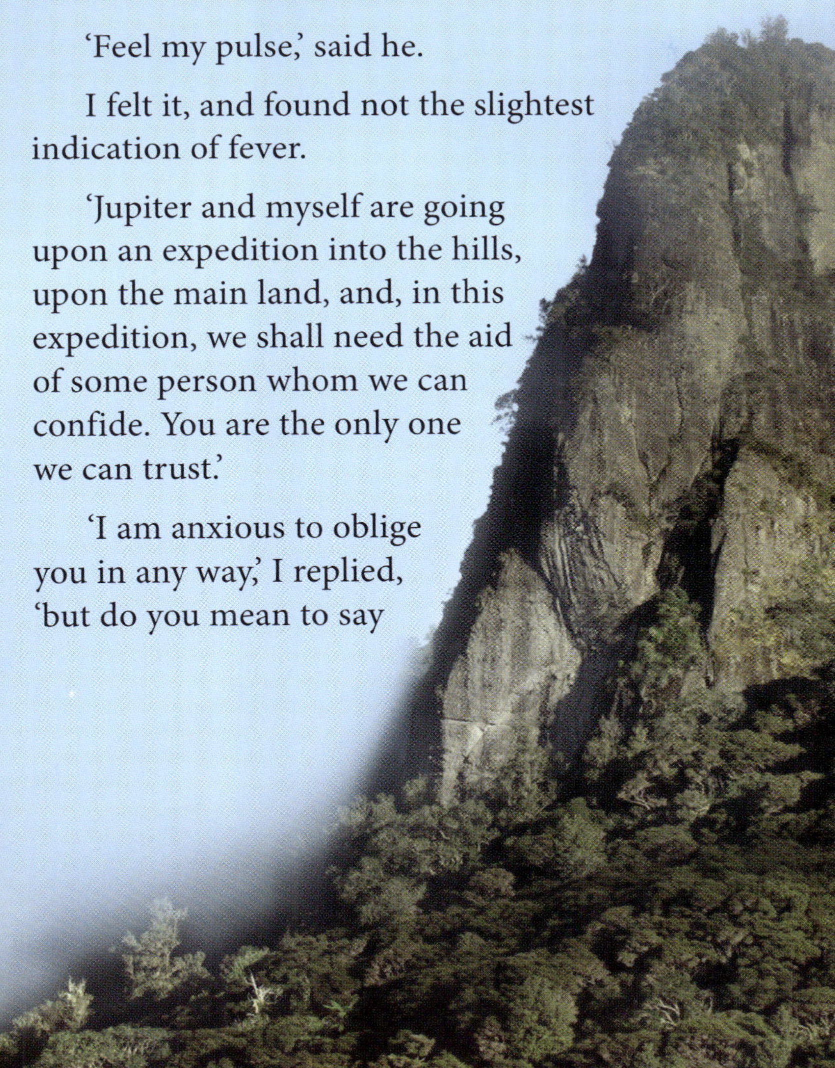

that this beetle has any connection with your planned expedition?'

'It has.'

'Then, Legrand, I cannot become a party to such absurd proceeding.'

'Well then, we shall have to try it by ourselves.'

'Try it by yourselves! The man is surely mad! How long do you propose to be absent?'

'Probably all night. We shall start immediately, and be back by sunrise.'

'And will you promise me, that when this freak of yours is over, and the bug business settled to your satisfaction, you will then return home and follow my advice and see your physician?'

'Yes; I promise; and now let us be off, for we have no time to lose.'

With a heavy heart, I accompanied my friend. We started off at about four o'clock— Legrand, Jupiter, the dog and myself. Jupiter had with him the scythe and spades. For my own part, I carried a couple of dark lanterns, while Legrand contented himself with the scarabaeus, which he carried attached to the end of a string; swinging it to and fro, with the air of a conjuror. When I observed this last, plain evidence of my friend's oddness of mind, I could scarcely refrain from tears.

We crossed the creek at the head of the island with a small boat and proceeded through a tract of desolate countryside. We journeyed for about two hours, and the sun was just setting when we reached an almost inaccessible densely wooded and rocky hill.

With Legrand's guidance, we cleared our way to the foot of an enormously tall tulip tree, which stood, with some eight or ten oaks but surpassed them all with its majesty. When we reached this tree, Legrand turned to

Jupiter, and asked him to climb the tree with the beetle in hand. Jupiter though staggered by the request, hesitatingly took hold of the extreme end of the string to which the beetle was attached and ascend the tree.

Jupiter, after one or two narrow escapes from falling, reached the first great fork, which was some sixty or seventy feet from the ground. Legrand, further instructed him to climb till the seventh branch and to report any strange sightings.

By this time what little doubt I might have entertained of my poor friend's insanity, was put finally at rest. I had no alternative but to conclude him mad, and I became seriously anxious about getting him home. While I was thinking about what was best to be done, Jupiter exclaimed that he had found a skull nailed to the branch. Legrand, instructed Jupiter to drop the beetle through the left eye of the skull, while holding the end of the string.

Although Jupiter could not be seen, the beetle, which he had let descend, was now visible at the end of the string, and glistened, like a globe of burnished gold, in the last rays of the setting sun. Legrand immediately took the scythe, and cleared with it a circular space, three or four yards in diameter, just beneath the bug. Having accomplished this, he ordered Jupiter to hand over the beetle and come down from the tree.

Driving a peg into the ground, at the precise spot where the beetle fell, Legrand attached a tape measure to a tree trunk and unrolled it until it reached the peg and continued till it reached fifty feet. There, he drove a second peg in the ground and drew a circle, about four feet in diameter around it. Taking now a spade himself, and giving one each to Jupiter and me, Legrand begged us to start digging as quickly as possible.

I was annoyed and puzzled, but I dragged myself to dig with a good will so that I can sooner convince him of the fallacy of the opinions he entertained.

The lanterns having been lit, we were drawn to our digging for almost two hours. Without much conversation we continued except for the growing excitement of the dog, which was evident from the noisy yelping, posing a threat to his master's task. Jupiter tied the dog's mouth up with one of his suspenders, and then returned, with a grave chuckle, to his task.

We had reached a depth of five feet, and yet there were no signs of treasure. Legrand, however, wiped his brow thoughtfully and began again. We went to the farther depth of two feet. Still nothing appeared. The gold-seeker with the bitterest disappointment proceeded, slowly and reluctantly, to put on his coat, which he had thrown off at the beginning of his labour. Jupiter, at a signal from his master, began to gather up his tools. This done, and the dog having been untied, we turned in profound silence towards home.

We had taken, perhaps, a dozen steps in this direction, when, with a loud oath, Legrand strode up to Jupiter, and seized him by the collar. The astonished man opened his eyes and mouth fully, let fall the spades, and fell upon his knees.

'You scoundrel,' said Legrand, hissing out the syllables from between his clenched teeth. 'You evil villain! Speak, I tell you! Answer me this instant, which is your left eye?'

'Oh, my golly, Massa Will! Is this not my left eye?' roared the terrified Jupiter, placing his hand upon his right organ of vision.

'I thought so! I knew it! Hurrah!' said Legrand, letting Jupiter go, much to his astonishment.

Legrand, again led us back, changing the spot where the beetle fell, to a spot about three inches westward of its former position. Adopting the same method as earlier, a spot was indicated, which was several yards, from the point at which we had been digging. We again set to work with the spades. After an hour and a half of digging, we were again interrupted by the violent howling of the dog. He leaped into the hole, tore up the ground frantically with his claws and in few seconds uncovered a mass of human bones, forming two complete skeletons, along with several buttons of metal, and what appeared to be the dust of decayed woollen. Further digging upturned the blade of a large Spanish knife and some loose pieces of gold and silver coin.

We now worked in earnest, and never did I pass ten minutes of more intense excitement. Finally, we unearthed a wooden chest of three feet and a half long, three feet broad, and two and a half feet deep. It was much too heavy to lift even for the three of us, together. Luckily, the sole fastenings of the lid consisted of two sliding bolts, which we drew back to find a treasure of incalculable value gleaming before us.

I shall not pretend to describe the feelings with which I gazed. Amazement was, of course, predominant. Legrand appeared exhausted with excitement, and spoke very few words. Jupiter seemed stupefied and repented for his former distrust of the bug.

We, finally, lightened the box by removing two-thirds of its contents to raise it from the hole. The articles taken out were deposited among the bushes, and the dog was left to guard them until our return. We then hurriedly headed home with the chest and reached at one o'clock in the morning. We rested until two, and start for the hills immediately after supper. A few minutes before four we arrived at the pit, and again set out for the hut, depositing our treasures at the first streaks of dawn.

We were now very tired but the intense excitement denied us peaceful rest and after some three or four hours of sleep, we arose, to examine our treasure.

The chest had been full to the brim, and we found ourselves possessed of even vaster wealth

than we had at first supposed. We estimated the value of coins—Spanish, French, German and English—at 4,50,000 dollars; and count 100 and 10 large diamonds; 18 rubies of remarkable brilliancy; 310 emeralds; 21 sapphires and an opal. Besides all this, there was a vast quantity of solid gold ornaments; nearly 200 massive finger and ear rings; rich chains; 83 very large and heavy crucifixes; 5 gold censers of great value; richly ornamented golden punch-bowl and many other smaller articles which I cannot recollect. The weight of these valuables exceeded 350 pounds and in this estimate, I had not included 197 superb gold watches. We expected the entire contents of the chest, that night, at a million and a half dollars.

Legrand, finally sensing my impatience for an explanation entered into a full detail of all the circumstances connected with it.

'You remember,' said he, 'the night when I handed you the rough sketch I had made of the scarabaeus. Your opinion about my drawing skills irritated me—for I am considered a good artist— and, therefore, when you handed me the scrap of paper, I was about to crumple it up and throw it angrily into the fire.'

'The scrap of paper, you mean,' said I.

'No; although it had the appearance of paper, I discovered it to be a piece of very thin parchment. It was quite dirty, you remember. Well, as I was in the very act of crumpling it up, my glance fell upon the sketch at which you had been looking, and to my astonishment, I saw the figure of a death's-head right where I had made the drawing of the beetle. For a moment, I was too much amazed to think with accuracy. I then took a candle and proceeded to scrutinize the paper more closely. Upon turning it over, I saw my own sketch upon the reverse, just as I had made it. I was surprised at the really remarkable coincidence that there was a skull upon the other side of the paper, immediately beneath my figure of the scarabaeus and that this skull, not only in outline, but in size, so closely resemble my drawing. I was certain that there had been no drawing on the paper when I made my sketch of the scarabaeus, for I recollected looking at both sides, in search of the cleanest spot. I arose at once, and putting the paper securely away, dismissed all farther reflection until I should be alone.

'When you had gone, and when Jupiter was fast asleep, I undertook a more methodical investigation of the affair. In the first place I considered the manner in which the paper had come into my possession. The spot where we discovered the scarabaeus was on the coast of the main land. Upon my taking hold of it, it gave me a sharp bite, which caused me to let it drop. Jupiter, with his accustomed caution, before seizing the insect, looked for a leaf, or something of that nature, by which to take hold of it. It was at this moment that his eyes, and mine also, fell upon

the scrap of paper. It was lying half buried in the sand, a corner sticking up. Near the spot where we found it, I observed the remnants of an old shipwreck.'

'On our way home, we met Lieutenant G—, and I showed him the insect to which he begged me to lend him and unconsciously, I must have deposited the paper in my own pocket.

'No doubt you will think me fanciful—but I had already established a kind of connection. I had put together two links of a great chain. There was a shipwreck on a seacoast, and not far from it was a paper with a skull depicted on it. The skull, or death's-head, is the well-known emblem of the pirate.

'But,' I interrupted, 'you say that the skull was not upon the paper when you made the drawing of the beetle. How then do you trace any connection between the boat and the skull?

'Ah, hereupon turns the whole mystery; since you did not draw the skull, and no one else was present to do it. Then it was not done by human agency. Nevertheless it was done.

'Just as I gave you the paper, you were interrupted by the dog and while you were attending to the dog, the paper fell close to the fire.

The heat from the fire, I reasoned was the agent in bringing to light the image of the skull on the paper. You are well aware that chemical preparations exist by means of which it is possible to write on either paper or vellum, so that the characters shall become visible only when subjected to heat.

'Later, I kindled a fire, and heat up the paper. A faint figure of a goat became visible; however a closer look convinced me that it was an image of a kid.'

'Ha! Ha!' said I, 'to be sure I have no right to laugh at you after the treasure but you are not about to establish a third link in your chain — pirates, you know, have nothing to do with goats.'

'But I have just said that the figure was not that of a goat, but a kid,' said Legrand. 'You may have heard of one Captain Kidd, a well-known pirate. I then inspect the paper more attentively for more information with a sudden hope of vast good fortune awaiting. I recalled the thousand vague rumours about immense wealth buried, somewhere on the Atlantic coast, by Kidd and his associates. I had a feeling that the paper involved a lost record of the place of deposit.'

'But how did you proceed?'

'I held the paper again to the fire but nothing appeared. I now thought it possible that the coating of dirt might have something to do with the failure; so I carefully rinsed the paper by pouring warm water over it and reheat it. And, to my inexpressible joy, found it spotted, in several places, with what appeared to be figures arranged in lines, the whole was just as you see it now.'

Here Legrand, having re-heated the paper, hand it over to me. The following characters were rudely traced, in a red tint, between the death's-head and the goat:

```
53++!305))6*;4826)4+.)4+);806*;48!8`60))85;]8*:+

*8!83(88)5*!; 46(;88*96*?;8)* +(;485);5*!2:*+ (;4956*

2(5*-4)8`8*; 4069285);)6 !8)4++;1(+9;48081;8:8+ 1;4

8!85;4)485!528806*81(+9;48;(88;4(+?3 4;48)4+;161;:

188;+?;
```

'But,' said I, returning him the slip, 'I am as much in the dark as ever.'

'You see,' said Legrand, 'these characters form a cipher with meaning hidden in code.'

'And you really solved it?'

'Readily; I have solved other puzzles ten thousand times more difficult than this. It was a simple substitution cipher and I assumed the hidden message to be in English as the pun on Kidd's name was in English. I counted the frequency of the symbols and used them to solve the cipher, which revealed the message to be:

"A good glass in the bishop's hostel in the devil's seat—twenty-one degrees and thirteen minutes—northeast and by north—main branch seventh limb east side— shoot from the left eye of the death's-head—a bee-line from the tree through the shot fifty feet out."

'For the next few days, I made diligent inquiry, in the neighbourhood of Sullivan's island and found out that Bishop's hostel was related to an old family named Bessop. I further discovered that there exists a Bessop's castle named by the family, which was neither a castle, nor a tavern but a high rock. I was directed to the place by an old lady and as I climb up and look around, a narrow ledge in the eastern face of the rock caught my attention.

This ledge projected about eighteen inches, and was not more than a foot wide. I made no doubt that here was the 'devil's-seat' referred to in the message, and now I seemed to grasp the full secret of the riddle.

'The "good glass," I knew, could only imply a telescope; for the word "glass" is rarely employed in any other sense by seamen. Knowing that a telescope was to be used and that the rest of the phrases were intended as directions, I hurried home excitedly, procured a telescope and returned to the rock.

'I let myself down to the ledge, and found that it was impossible to retain a seat on it unless in one particular position. Then I proceeded to use the glass. Of course, the "twenty-one degrees and thirteen minutes" could only mean the elevation above the visible horizon, since the horizontal direction was clearly indicated by the words, "northeast and by north". This latter direction I at once established by means of a pocket compass; then, as I moved it cautiously up or down, my attention was captured by a circular rift in the foliage of a large tree that surpassed all other trees nearby. Adjusting the focus of the telescope, I again looked at the rift, and to my utter astonishment saw a human skull.

'I was now suddenly hopeful of solving the mystery; for the phrase "main branch, seventh limb, east side", could refer only to the position of the skull on the tree, while "shoot from the left eye of the death's-head" was to drop a bullet from the left eye of the skull. A beeline or a straight line, drawn "from the tree through the shot," (or the spot where the bullet fell) and from there extended to a distance of fifty feet, would indicate a definite point—and beneath this point I knew that a deposit of value lay hidden.'

'All this,' I said, 'is exceedingly clear and very clever. When you left the Bishop's Hostel, what then?'

'I turned homewards after carefully noting down the locations of the tree. The instant that I left "the devil's seat", the circular rift, however vanished; nor could I get a glimpse of it afterwards. I was convinced that the rift was visible only from the narrow ledge on the rock.

'In the meantime, Jupiter sensed the change in my behaviour and kept a watch on all my activities. But, on the next day, I went out unnoticed and went into the hills in search of the tree. When I came home at night Jupiter proposed to give me a flogging. With the rest of the adventure I believe you are as well acquainted as myself.'

'I suppose,' said I, 'you missed the spot, in the first attempt at digging through Jupiter's stupidity in letting the bug fall through the right instead of the left of the skull.'

'Precisely. This mistake made a difference of about two inches and a half in the "shot"—that is to say, in the position of the peg nearest the tree; the error, however small in the beginning, increased as we proceeded with the line, and by the time we had gone fifty feet, threw us quite off the scent.'

'I presume the idea of the skull, of letting fall a bullet through the skull's eye—was suggested to Kidd by the piratical flag.'

'Perhaps so; or maybe it was common sense. To be visible from the devil's-seat, it was necessary that the object, if small, should be white; and there is nothing like human skull for retaining and even increasing its whiteness under exposure to all changes of weather.'

'But your exaggerations, and your conduct in swinging the beetle—how excessively odd! I was sure you were mad. And why did you insist on letting fall the bug, instead of a bullet, from the skull?'

'Why, to be frank, I felt somewhat annoyed by your evident suspicions regarding

my sanity, and so resolved to punish you quietly, in my own way, by intentionally overacting. For this reason, I swung the beetle and let it fall from the tree. An observation of yours about its great weight suggested the latter idea.'

'I understand, and now there is only one point which puzzles me: the skeletons found in the hole.'

'That is a question I am no more able to answer than you. There seems, however, only one realistic answer. It is clear that Kidd while hiding this treasure must have had assistance in the labour. However, after it was done, he may have thought it necessary to remove all participants in his secret. Perhaps a couple of blows were sufficient, while his assistants were busy in the pit; perhaps it required a dozen—who shall tell?'

The Mill on the Floss
George Eliot

It was a cold, but bright February morning. Mr and Mrs Tulliver, the miller and his wife were sitting by the fire in their home, the Dorlcote Mill. It stood on the river Ripple, a small tributary of the river Floss. The nearest town to the Mill was St Ogg's. Mill that used to be the family home for the Tullivers for many years.

Mr Tulliver was interested to send his young son Tom to a good school at Midsummer for further education, so that Tom's intellectual knowledge could help him in legal matters in future.

'I want to give Tom a good education. That is what I was thinking of when I gave notice for him to leave the academy at Ladyday. I want Tom to be a bit of a scholar, so he might be up for the tricks of these lawyers,' said Mr Tulliver.

Mrs Tulliver said that she too did want him to go to a good school, but wanted that he should not be sent too far away because she would like to do things for him by way of sending food and clothes whenever he needed them.

Mr and Mrs Tulliver conversation dilly dallied around Tom and his education. Mr Tulliver thought that Tom was not bright and good as his sister Maggie in studies. Maggie was bright and pretty too. But for Mrs Tulliver Maggie was too stubborn and her long hair made her look like a pony.

The next day, Mr Riley, the auctioneer came to meet Tullivers. He was educated and qualified and seemed fit to advise the Tullivers on Tom's future. Mr Riley recommended a private tutor

named Reverend Stelling. He was an Oxford man. Stelling was a well-sized, broad-chested man and had large grey eyes. He also had a bold, bass voice.

For a short-term course, Tom was under the guidance of Rev Stelling yet before long, it was time to return. Mr Tulliver went to take him back. Maggie was not allowed to accompany them

because of her mother's objections. But she was very happy with the news that Tom was coming home.

'Yap, Yap, Tom is coming home,' she said, running round and round the garden.

Soon, Tom arrived to the delight of his sister and mother.

It was the Easter weekend. The Tullivers organized a family party wherein they invited all their aunts and uncles. Mr Tullivers had three sisters, all of them were married. Mrs Glegg, Mrs Pullet and Mrs Deane. The party turned out to be interesting.

The next day, the Tullivers went to farmhouse to visit Mr and Mrs Pullet. Mr Pullet was a farmer and he had many pets—peacocks, guinea fowls, pigeons, a magpie, a goat and a huge mastiff. The mastiff was a bulldog and big and enormous like a lion. Tom wandered around in the farm.

Tom and Maggie would often quarrel on the most petty issue. But by the end of the day, they would eventually make up.

Time passed by, soon the time had come for Tom to leave for school. Maggie was very sad.

Tom was sent to King's Lorton School this time for a full course. In the previous academy, life was not a difficult problem. There were many fellows to play with, and Tom was good at active games. This had become an important part of his personality.

In his new school, however, he was extremely unhappy; here he had no boys to play with, he spent most of his time in loneliness. Moreover, Tom was not good at studies and he found Rev Walter Stelling's method of teaching difficult to understand. But Stelling was determined and firm, to educate Tom in his first term. Tom felt lonely day by day. He yearned for a companion. Finally, he got a break when Mr Tulliver and Maggie visited Tom in his school.

'Well, my boy,' Mr Tulliver said to Tom. 'School seems to agree with you.'

'I don't think the things are going well,' Tom said, quite honestly. 'Mr Stelling makes me do Euclid—it is all greek to me, I think. I get a headache.'

'Euclid, what is that?' asked Mr Tulliver.

'Oh, I have no idea. A book of definitions, triangles and things. It makes no sense to me,' said Tom.

'Go on, you must do what your master tells you,' Mr Tulliver said.

'I will help you,' Maggie said, intervening in the conservation between the father and son.

'Girls cannot learn Euclid and geometry,' said Tom.

'But I can stay and help you,' Maggie said.

'You can stay for a fortnight, and then Mr Tulliver can come and fetch you,' said Mrs Stelling.

So, it was decided that Maggie would stay with Tom for a fortnight. Maggie stayed for a fortnight, became good friends with Mr Stelling. They often discussed on a variety of subjects. Soon Maggie had to leave. Tom missed his sister, when she returned home. Soon, Tom's first quarter came to an end. At last, Tom was happy to come home. With snowy hair and ruddy face, he reached home for Christmas. On the Christmas day, the house was decorated with holly and ivy leaves. The roasted turkey and plum pudding indeed tasted very good.

But there was tension in the household too. Mr Tulliver was cross and cranky. One Mr Pivart had moved into the vicinity. He had plans to irrigate the land with water from the Ripple. This meant that he would construct dykes and irrigation canals. This would affect water supply to the mill. This could be disastrous for the mill and people too.

Mr Tulliver was thinking of going to the law, but Mrs Tulliver was against it because Mr Pivart was a rich man and he could use his power and money to influence the court's judgment. Moreover, he was being forced by Wakem, a lawyer to file the case and Mr Tulliver had found fresh evidence stating that Mr Pivart and Wakem were thick friends.

Before long, Tom's holidays came to end. It was a cold, January morning, when with a sad heart, he went back to school.

'Well, Tulliver, it is great to see you again,' said Mr Stelling. 'Take off your coat and come to the sitting room.'

There he saw Philip Wakem, Wakem's son. Tom had seen Philip in St Ogg, but never made friends with him. He hated having a crippled boy as his friend. He was sitting and making drawings of donkeys, spaniels and partridges.

'I wish I could draw Iike you,' said Tom. 'Where did you learn to draw?'

'I never learned drawing,' said Philip.

'How old are you? I am fifteen,' said Philip.

'I am not fourteen yet,' said Tom. 'I wish Mr Stelling would allow us to go for fishing together.'

'Oh, I don't like fishing. I think people look fools sitting and watching the fishing line,' snapped back Philip.

So this time Tom was not lonely, and Philip Wakem had taken admission under Mr Stelling. The two boys got on well.

The two became good friends. With each passing day, a remarkable difference and improvement was coming in Tom's studies. It was somewhat due to Philip and to some extent Mr Stelling.

Mr Poulter was employed for Tom's exercises and military drill. So, his physique also underwent a massive change. Mr Poulter had fought against Napoleon armies and cut off heads of many Frenchmen.

Maggie arrived again. She was overwhelmed with Philip, as she always had a soft spot

for handicapped children. Philip too had a penchant for dark eyes, which Maggie was gifted with.

Time passed by, Tom entered the fifth half-year. Till he turned sixteen, he studied and stayed at King's Lorton. Maggie was growing up with her cousin Lucy as her companion at a boarding school. She would often write letters to Tom, wherein she always sent her love for Philip. Tom, then, was looking quite different from those days in his last term. He had become tall, good looking, polite and well-mannered—and not but the least, confident about himself.

He had not heard from home for a long time, however, one day Maggie appeared. She looked quite sullen. Tom knew something was wrong. Their father had lost the lawsuit, which meant everything they owned from the mill to the furniture was now Mr Pivart's property.

Taking leave from Mr Stelling, he decided to leave for home. Suddenly everything had changed. There was no place that he could call home.

When Mr Tulliver came to know he had lost everything, he comforted himself thinking that he could always borrow money to pay off his dues. This was when he thought of Mr Furley. Mr Furley had taken a loan from him to buy some land and he could ask him to pay what he still owed him. This amount could help him to overcome his financial difficulties.

Mr Tulliver set off on his horse to meet Mr Furley. But on his way, a clerk told him that Furley had sold his land and insecurities to Wakem. It was too much for Mr Tulliver to

bear. He fell off from his horse and became unconscious.

When the siblings reached home, their father was unconscious and was unable to recognize anyone.

'All the time, I kept on telling him not to go to the law,' Mrs Tulliver cried. 'What more I could do?'

'Don't worry,' said Tom. 'Soon I would be able to find job and earn some money.'

Maggie, who was listening to the conversation between her mother and brother, felt extremely bad.

She said, 'Mother, how can you talk for father like this?'

Turning to Tom she spoke, 'Tom, you should not let anybody talk about your father like that, at the moment when he is lying helpless, unable to defend himself.'

Choking with grief and anger, she left the room. She felt very sad that now everybody would blame him.

The next day, Tom went to meet Uncle Deane to get some employment. He was hopeful that Mr Deane would help him find a suitable job and help him family in this difficulty.

But unfortunately, the meeting did not go well. The subjects that Tom had studied—Latin, Greek, Roman, History and Euclid's geometry were not of any significance or use in Mr Deane's firm, as the firm handled auditing accounts. Soon, Tom returned home disappointed.

On a dark December day, all the household furniture of Tullivers was taken by the strangers. Mr Tulliver was subconsciously aware of what was going on.

One day in the evening, Tom had an unexpected guest at home. He was an old village friend of his, Bob Jakin. Tom had long ago given a pocket knife to him, and whenever he used it, he remembered him. He had come to know of Tom's financial difficulty. He had earned ten gold coins by helping the owner to put out a fire at his mill. He had spent nine coins to buy things for his mother and was left with one, Hence, he had come to give it to Tom. Tom was touched by the gesture, but refused to take the coin. He wanted to earn and get back what he possessed and not depend on charity.

Tom embraced Bob. They soon parted.

By the end of the second week of January, both the Dorlcotte Mill and land were bought by Wakem. On the other hand, the doctor affirmed Mr Tulliver would regain his normal health soon. When he did recover, he found that he was bankrupt and things would never be the same again.

With nothing left, Mrs Tuliver suggested Mr Tulliver to take up the job with Wakem. Tom was reluctant and said, 'I have got a job in Guest and Co's warehouses which pay me a pound a week. This is not enough but things will improve as time passes by.'

But Mr Tulliver took the tough decision, and decided to take up employment under Wakem and serve him like an honest man. Wakem had promised a salary of thirty shillings a week and a horse to ride in the market.

Around three years later, Maggie was sitting by the window, when she saw Wakem entering the yard with his black horse. He was accompanied by Philip Wakem, who had come back home after a long stay abroad.

Maggie would often go for long walk in the woods. The most frequent place she visited was the Red Deeps. One day, as she was walking and enjoying fresh air and sunlight, she thought someone was following her, she turned back and saw Philip Wakem.

'You startled me, Philip,' said Maggie. 'Did you come to meet me?'

'I have been watching you. I made a picture of you when you came to stay at the school,' said Philip.

This was the beginning of a beautiful relationship between Philip and Maggie. But Maggie could not make up her mind; she was confused between her father and Philip. Meanwhile, Tom had started to earn some money. He had become more confident now. One day, Bob Jakin, his old friend came up with a business proposal. He had to export some cargo to foreign countries. But he needed goods to export them to foreign countries. So, he turned to Uncle Gregg. He needed twenty pounds in return for 5 per cent of profits. Uncle Gregg agreed. The business started off well. Soon the business grew.

Maggie's relationship also started growing with Philip. Soon, Tom got to know that there was something amiss between Philip and Maggie. One day, while on one of the walks with Philip, Tom caught Maggie. Tom gave a warning to Maggie, 'Either you leave Philip or I will tell everything to father.'

It was a tough choice, but she decided to leave Philip for her father. That was the end of the relationship.

Three weeks later, Tom reached home from his day's work. He said to his father, 'Father, please bring the tin saving box from my bedroom.'

Mr Tulliver brought the box and started counting the money.

'Only a hundred and ninety three pounds,' he said. 'We still need three hundred—it will take time to save that. You have to bury me first.'

'No father,' Tom said, 'you will be able to see your debts paid.'

One day, Mr Tulliver was spreading manure on the field.

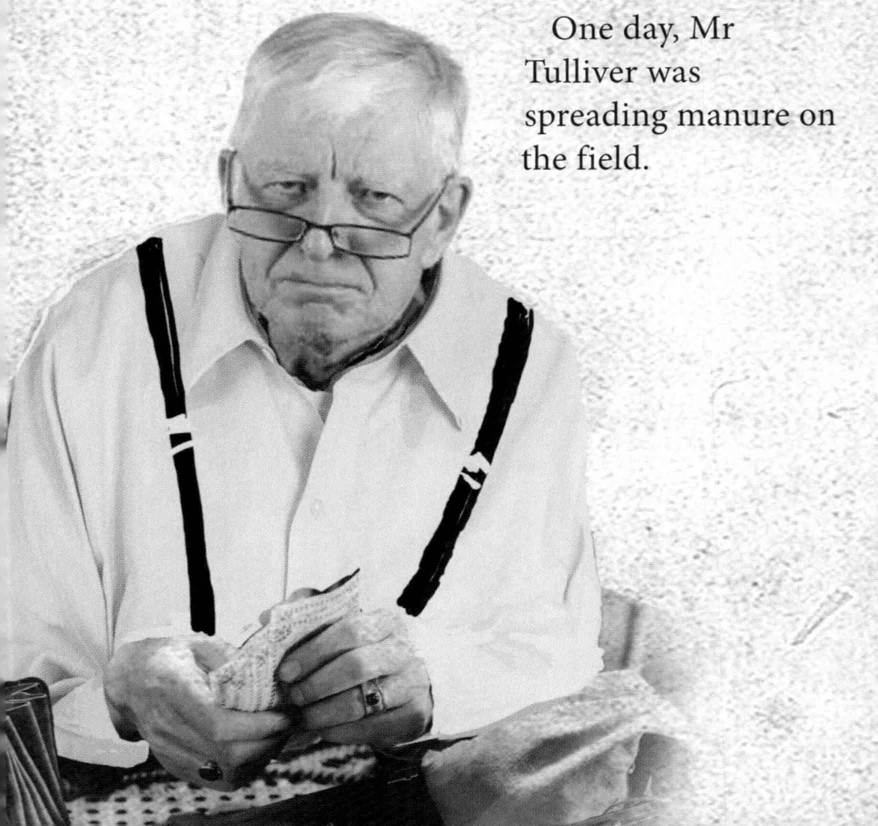

'Tulliver, what a fool you are,' said Wakem, who was on his black horse. 'How many times have I told not to do this?'

It was hard for Tulliver. He could not take it anymore.

'Get someone else to do your farming,' Tulliver replied.

'You may leave tomorrow from the premises,' shot back Wakem.

Tulliver got angry. He prodded his horse and lifted his whip. Wakem's horse got alarmed and threw the rider. Before Wakem could rise, Mr Tulliver flogged him on his back.

Listening to the noise, Maggie rushed out and tried to stop her father. As she was trying to drag her father, he suffered a stroke and died.

Meanwhile, Tom came out. Both sister and brother hugged and wept together.

Maggie went to stay with the Deanes to recover from the tragedy. She felt happy in the company of Lucy Deane, who had Stephen Guest, heir to the flourishing firm of Guest and Co, as her companion.

One day, a conversation was taking place between Lucy and Stephen, when Philip Wakem's name cropped up. Lucy wanted to invite Philip for a meeting. Maggie felt uneasy and remembered the promise she had given to her brother. She decided to tell Lucy of her affair with Philip Wakem and later talk to her brother.

Maggie met Lucy after Stephen left and narrated her the story. She felt great relief after speaking out and telling her story.

Lucy advised her see to Tom. She went to meet Tom, who was staying at his friend's Bob's place.

'I want you to release me from my promise about Philip Wakem,' she said. 'I would be meeting him in a day or two.'

'When our father was alive I felt it was great need to bind you to protect my father and you from disgracing yourself. Now I leave upon you; I still have the same feelings, as I had; if you think Philip as your lover, then you need to give up on me,' said Tom coldly.

'I don't wish too—I like to be friends with him, till the time he will be there. I soon shall go away to another job. Besides, Lucy wishes too,' said Maggie.

Tom said, 'I shouldn't mind at you seeing him often at my uncle's place. I want to be a good brother to you.'

Maggie was relieved. She went back happily. She looked forward for her meeting with Philip in the evening.

But Philip did not come for the meeting, he had perhaps gone for a sketching trip and it was not clear when he would return.

Actually, he returned after a fortnight, with Lucy's notes awaiting him.

In the meantime, a relationship was developing between Stephen and Maggie. Stephen was taking great interest in Maggie's affairs and Maggie found him attractive, too. Both of them were conscious of the other's presence but hardly spoke.

Interestingly, while Stephen and Maggie was becoming closer, Philip came back. After a few moments, ice was broken; and both of them clasped their hands together as Maggie admitted, 'I told my brother that I wish to see you. He did not raise any objections.'

'We can be friends now, at least now,' replied Philip.

'Won't your father object?' asked Maggie.

'There are some things I resist. And this will be definitely one of them,' said Philip.

'There is nothing that can prevent us from being friends. But as you know I would be leaving for another job,' said Maggie.

'Is it necessary to go?' asked Philip.

'Yes, I must go. Though my brother is really good, I cannot be dependent on him. I cannot expect that he would bear me for long,' she said.

Soon Stephen entered the scene and he shook hands with Philip. After some banter, Stephen started to sing. Maggie was overwhelmed by his singing and could not hide her feelings.

Philip knew instantly that there was something going on between the two of them.

'It was natural for a man to fall in love with Maggie,' he thought.

As the days passed by, Stephen and Maggie were coming closer. Stephen visited the Deanes to meet Maggie's, when he knew Lucy would not be there. Maggie feeling towards Stephen was also becoming stronger with each passing day. She decided that the only solution was to go away. Her old school mistress help found a job of a governess to three motherless children.

She went to stay with Aunt Gritty Moss's house to escape from Stephen. But Stephen could not resist himself and came straight to meet her in the house. He told her that he loved her passionately.

She said, 'Stephen, think of Lucy, how unfair it would be for her, if we carried on like this. Don't provoke me. Help me! Help me!'

'Dear, I will bear anything you wish,' he said. 'One last kiss before we go from each other.'

Maggie kissed Stephen and hurried back to the house.

About a week later, Maggie returned to St Ogg to spend time with Lucy before she took up the post of a governess. Stephen also tried hard to keep away from her. But it did not last long.

Philip had become an occasional visitor to the house, and it was on one of these days that Lucy said, 'I think we four should go for boating till Maggie is here.'

So, a programme was made. Four of them— Lucy, Philip, Stephen and Maggie set off for a sea trip. It so happened, at the last minute, Lucy and Philip backed out, which left Stephen and Maggie on their own.

Once on board, their yacht glided rapidly, thanks to the fast flowing tide. They went too far away and before they realized it was impossible to come back with the tide. Soon, they saw a small ship coming after them.

'If this ship is going to Mudport, we must go on board; it will be best and safe way to return home,' Stephen said.

When the ship came near, Stephen chatted with the captain and thankfully the captain agreed. They settled themselves on a couch with cushions. The two lovers were beside each other and spent the night together.

The next morning, Maggie felt miserable and was consumed with a feeling of guilt. She felt that the time had come to part away. She had betrayed her trusted people—Lucy and Tom.

She decided to take up a job faraway from people she loved.

'Dear, how can you go back without marrying me,' said Stephen. 'You don't know what will people say.'

'People will believe me. Lucy will forgive, Stephen please let me go,' said Maggie.

Stephen realized that it was all over; and he let her go.

On the afternoon of the fifth day from which Stephen and Maggie had left St Ogg, Tom was standing outside Dorlcote Mill.

Tom had brought the mill back. He had fulfilled his father's wish. By his sincerity and hard work, he had brought back the old

respectability of the Tullivers. But Tom's face, as he was standing, had no happiness and no triumph on it. There was no news of her sister since Bob Jakin had come back in the ship from Mudport and that she had seen her land the vessel with Mr Stephen Guest. Tom's mind expected the worse, not death, but disgrace. As he was walking, he saw a dark-eyed figure approaching him. He paused, trembling with disgust and indignation. He was very angry with Maggie.

'Tom, I have come back to you, to tell you everything,' said Maggie, who had finally arrived.

'You cannot live with me. You have disgraced us all. You are wicked and a curse to your friends,' he said.

'Tom, I am not guilty as you believe. I was carried too far in the boat. I've returned as soon as I can,' said Maggie.

'I can't believe you anymore. You have been in a secret relationship with Mr Stephen Guest, your cousin's lover, as you were with Philip. He went to fetch you from Aunt Moss's house. You have cheated your cousin. Go and see what you have done to Lucy—she is ill and can't speak,' Tom said.

Maggie was stunned. How could she vindicate herself?

'Tom, whatever I have done, I will make amends for that. I want to keep away from doing wrong again.'

'You shall not come under my roof. You are the symbol of disgrace. Your sight is hateful to me,' said Tom.

Mrs Tulliver was listening to the conversation between the sister and brother. She put her arms around Maggie and said, 'I will go with you.'

The news that Miss Tulliver had come back and that she had eloped to marry Mr Stephen had spread like wildfire in St Ogg.

Maggie and Mrs Tulliver stayed at Bob Jakin's house. After a few days, Mrs Tulliver came back to the mill, while Maggie decided to stay to find a job for herself.

A few days later, she received a letter from her friend Philip.

Dear Maggie,

May God help you, my loving Maggie, if every other person has failed to understand you, remember that I believe you. You will never be doubted by me.

Do not believe anyone, who says I am ill, because I am not seen outdoors. I have only had nervous headaches. I am still strong enough to obey any word which you tell me.

Yours, to the last,

Philip Wakem

After reading the letter, Maggie started sobbing. She pressed the letter to her heart. She was very happy that she had a true friend.

One evening, when she was sitting alone, she was visited by someone unexpected. It was Lucy. The face was there—but completely changed. Lucy threw her arms around Maggie's neck.

'God bless you for coming, Lucy.'

The sobs became thick from now onwards.

'Maggie, dear,' said Lucy. 'Don't be upset.'

Lucy was soothing Maggie with her gentle caress.

'I did not want to cheat you. I always felt miserable but I thought I would be able to overcome the feelings,' said Maggie.

'I know, dear,' said Lucy. 'I know you never had the intention to make me unhappy. It is misfortune that has come on us all. You had to bear more than I have; you gave him up—though it would have been hard on you.'

Both of them felt silent for a little while, they were sitting with clasped hands.

'Lucy, Stephen struggled too,' Maggie said after some time. 'He wanted to be true to you. He will surely come back to you. Forgive him, and then you will be happy.'

'I can't be you, Maggie; I can't…,' said Lucy.

Lucy trembled and became silent. It was getting late, Lucy had to leave. She rose and said, 'Well, I am going away on Friday, Maggie. When I come back, maybe I will be strong.'

'Lucy,' said Maggie. 'I pray to God I may never be the cause of sorrow to you ever again.'

Maggie pressed her hand.

'Maggie,' said Lucy in a low voice. 'You are better than I am.'

She left and said no more. But they embraced each other again.

In the second week of September, it was raining continuously. The old men in the town talked of sixty years ago when this kind of weather swept the bridge away and deserted the town.

In the higher counties up the floss, the completion of the harvest had been stalled.

In no time, the river was flooded. Soon the water reached the house. Maggie gave a call for the boats. It was total darkness.

'Oh, god where am I? Which is the way home,' she cried out. 'What is happening to my mother and brother at the mill?'

She heard Tom's voice from the wilderness.

'Get into the boat,' she said in a loud, piercing voice. But it was too late. The two were carried away by the flow of water and soon disappeared.

Nature mended and restored her ravages with her sunshine and human labour. The first autumn after the ravage was loaded and stuffed with golden corn stacks, while wharves and warehouses were teeming again with human voices eager to load and unload.

Nature revamps and refurbishes her destruction—but not all. The uprooted trees are not rooted gain, hills are left mutilated, if there is new growth, trees are not the same as the old and the hills sustain the past rending. To the eyes that have looked at the past, there is no meticulous repair.

Dorlcote Mill was rebuilt. And in the mill's churchyard, a tomb was erected. Soon after the flood, two bodies were found in tight embrace. The tombs bore the names of Tom and Maggie Tulliver. Below their names it was written—in their death they were not divided.

Other Titles *In The* Series

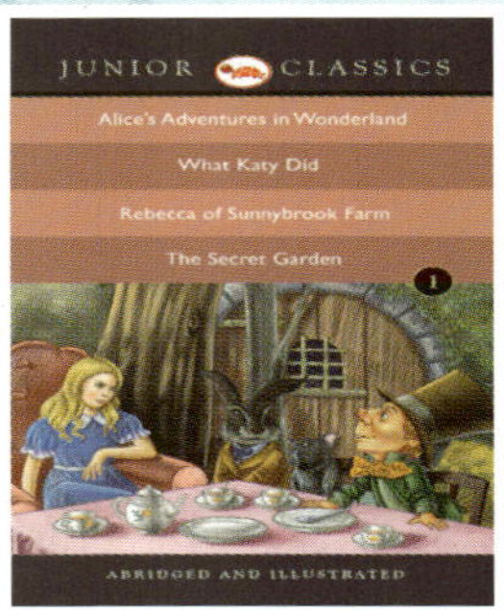

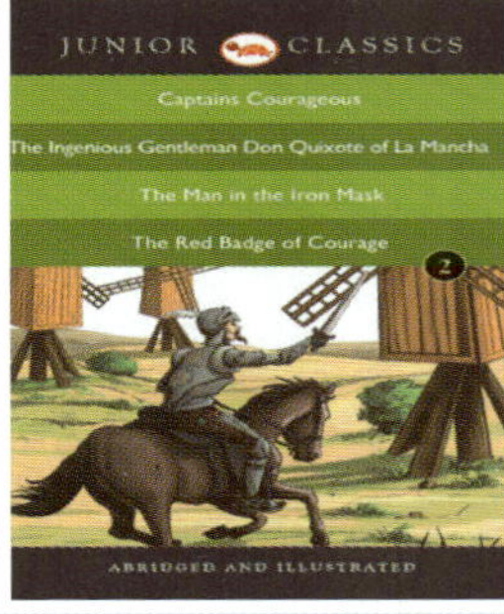

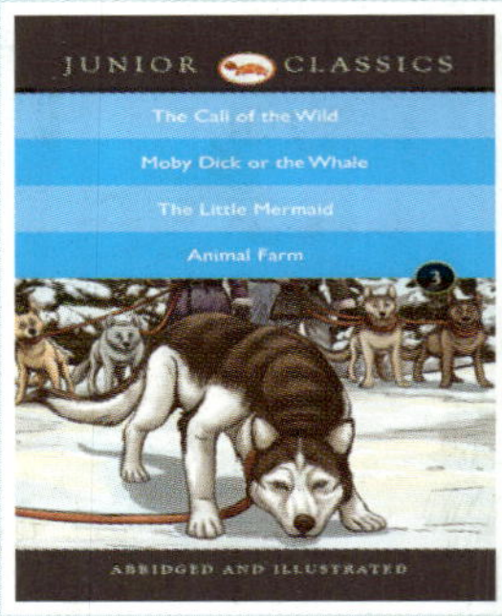

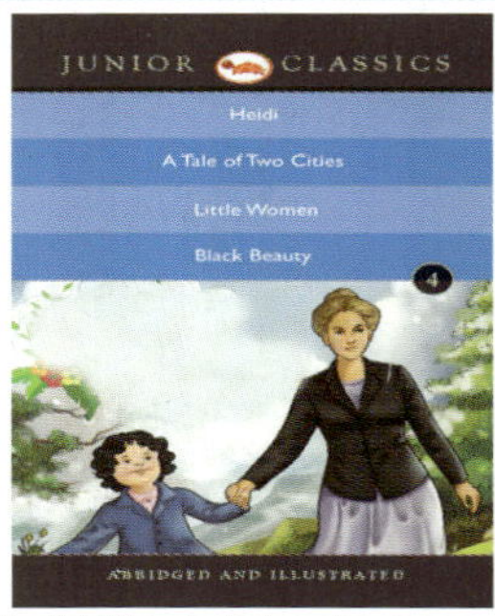

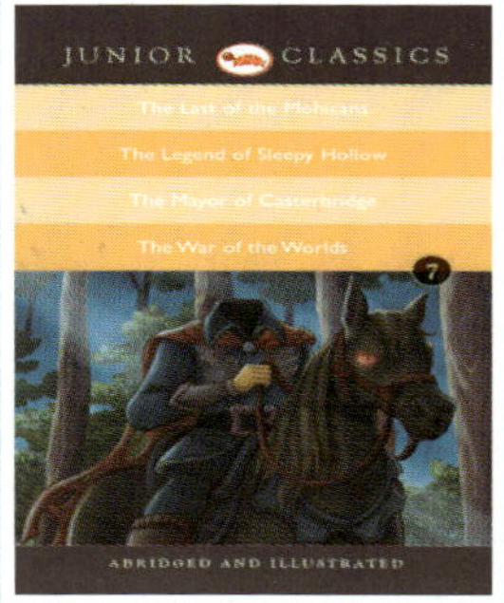

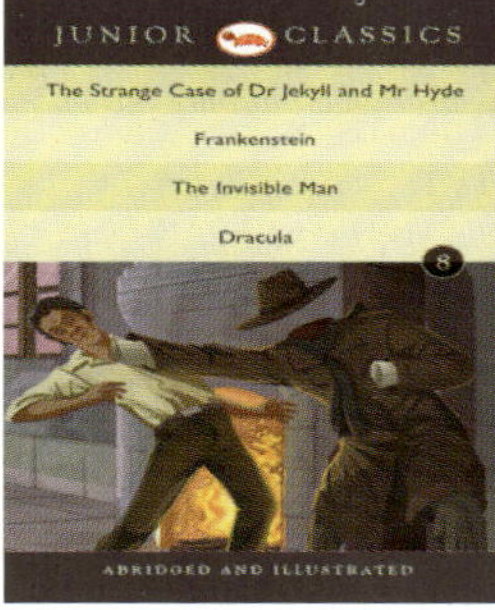

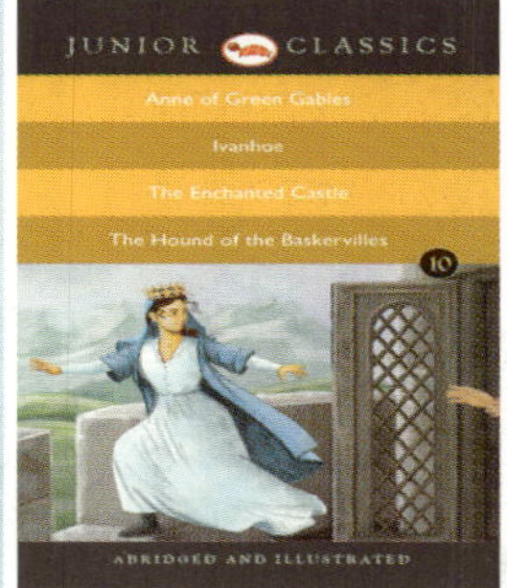